ase Files #4

# The No-Good Knight

Written by Jo Hurley

A
**LITTLE APPLE**
PAPERBACK

SCHOLASTIC INC.

New York  Toronto  London  Auckland  Sydney
Mexico City  New Delhi  Hong Kong  Buenos Air

No part of this publication may be reproduced in whole or in part, or stored in a retrieval system, or transmitted in any form or by any means, electronic, mechanical, photocopying, recording, or otherwise, without written permission of the publisher. For information regarding permission, write to Scholastic Inc., Attention: Permissions Department, 557 Broadway, New York, NY 10012.

ISBN 13: 978-0-545-00668-2

ISBN 10: 0-545-00668-6

Copyright © 2008 Hanna-Barbera. SCOOBY-DOO and all related characters and elements are trademarks of and © Hanna-Barbera.

Published by Scholastic Inc. All rights reserved.

SCHOLASTIC, LITTLE APPLE, and associated logos are trademarks and/or registered trademarks of Scholastic Inc.

Designed by Michael Massen

12  11  10  9  8  7  6  5  4  3  2  1          7  8  9  10  11/0

Special thanks to Duendes del Sur for cover and interior illustrations.

Printed in the U.S.A.

First printing, February 2008

Hi! I'm Velma Dinkley, and this is Daphne, Fred, Shaggy, and of course, Scooby-Doo. We're the gang from Mystery, Inc. and we're really glad you could join us. We've just come back from a super-tough case that might interest you. Won't you help us take a look at our case files — and help us analyze the clues?

Everything we saw at the scene of this mystery has been recorded on the following pages. You'll find notes, photographs, and puzzles to identify suspects and connect clues. When you're done, you should be able to unmask our mysterious No-Good Knight.

So sharpen your pencil, get out your magnifying glass, and turn the page for your first Case Files entry.

Smart sleuthing!

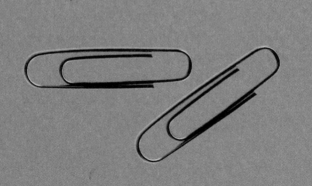

From the desk of
**Mystery, Inc.**

"Incredible!" Fred cried as he read the local paper. "It says here that the Ticklewell Feather Factory is closing."

"Jinkies!" I said. "That place is practically an institution around here. They make all the pillows in the area."

Shaggy groaned. "Like, pillow shmillow. Where's lunch?"

"Reah, reah!" Scooby said. His stomach growled on cue and he slurped at the air. "Runch!"

Daphne grabbed a tray of sandwiches from the kitchen, and the gang dove for the food. Well, Shaggy and Scooby dove. Within seconds, they'd eaten every last crust.

"Thanks for saving some for the rest of us," Daphne said, giggling. I had to laugh, too. I remember one time Shaggy and Scooby were so hungry they ate a bowl of waxed fruit.

But Fred wasn't laughing this time. He looked downright serious.

Ready, Set,

EAT! ↗

"I knew the Ticklewell family when I was little," Fred said. "That factory has been in their family for more than a century. They wouldn't just sell it out of the blue. Would they?"

"You're right," Daphne said. "Sounds like something strange is going on."

"Strange?" I asked, repeating the word. Strange was our code for "here comes a mystery!"

I was intrigued, so I grabbed the newspaper that Fred had been reading. Maybe it would tell us more about why the mansion was being sold.

"Rowroooooooo!" Scooby wailed. He rubbed his full belly.

"Like, I'm right there with you, Scoob. I'm about as stuffed as a . . ."

"Feather pillow?" cried Daphne.

Everyone laughed.

"Hold on!" I cried. I'd found something important in the back pages of the paper. I tore it out. "Read this!"

"There you go!" Daphne said. "Developers are moving in. That explains a lot."

# NEWSFLASH

Crank Construction announced plans to break ground on several new housing developments in the area. Proposed sites may include the Mile-High Marina and Ticklewell Manor.

Fred shook his head. "There must be something more than that."

"Wait!" I cried. "There is more! Check this out."

I held up another section of the newspaper.

## From Day to . . . Knight?

The chicken is fleeing the coop over at Ticklewell Feather Factory because the house is totally haunted! At least six witnesses report seeing a knight with red flashing eyes at the mansion.

"Wow," Daphne said. "A ghost? With red flashing eyes? Now that's a reason to get rid of the place. Scary!"

"I told you there was something else!" Fred cried.

"Like, do you think it really could be the spirit of Thaddeus Ticklewell?" Shaggy asked nervously.

"There's only one way to find out," I said.

Fred telephoned the lady of the house, Myrna Ticklewell. He asked if we could visit the mansion. Myrna was thrilled to hear from Fred after so many years. She said we could come over right away and that she'd tell us the rest of the story in person.

"The rest of the story?" I said. "Sounds interesting."

"Like, there's no way I'm going to some ghost factory," Shaggy moaned.

Scooby gulped. His paws were shaking.

I glared at them over the top of my glasses. "We're going," I said firmly.

"Nooooo way, Velm-ay!" Shaggy whined as Scooby crawled under the table and covered his eyes with both paws.

"Gee, it's too bad that you don't want to come," Daphne said sweetly, "because I just filled the Mystery Machine with a super supply of snack food. Now it'll just have to go to waste."

Shaggy's and Scooby's ears perked up. Before I could count to ten, they raced through the door and soon we were all in the van, hitting the road for Ticklewell Manor.

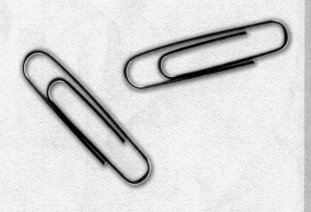

# Puzzle #1

The gang from Mystery, Inc. is on the move and ready for some serious sleuthing. Before you join us, you'll need to sharpen your ghost sensors with this triple-powered puzzle.

## Part One

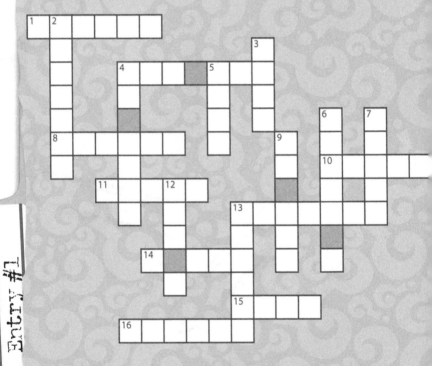

**ACROSS**
1. Are you _____ of the dark?
4. The boogie _____ lives under my bed
8. She wears cool scarves
10. Mystery, Inc. always investigates someplace _____
11. Eat this between meals
13. Person who may have committed a crime
14. She's the brains behind Mystery, Inc.
15. Meet the _____ (title of this puzzle)
16. Ruh roh, he's the dog

**DOWN**
2. The first "F" in BFF, or, who you hang out with
3. The leader of the gang
4. With 6 Down, the gang's wheels
5. Set this to catch someone
6. With 4 Down, the gang's wheels
7. Casper, the friendly _____
9. A dog does this to a cat
12. Pieces of information you gather to solve a crime
13. Like, he's the laid-back one

## Part Two

Write down all the letters from the shaded squares and then unscramble them to spell a mystery word that rhymes with hair.

___ ___ ___ ___ ___

## Part Three

In five steps, can you turn your mystery word into a snack? First, write down the mystery word on line one. Then, change one letter in that word to form a new word. Do it four more times until you get to the word SNACK. You can only change one letter at a time. Good luck!

1. ___ ___ ___ ___ ___
2. ___ ___ ___ ___ ___
3. ___ ___ ___ ___ ___
4. ___ ___ ___ ___ ___
5. ___ ___ ___ ___ ___

## Bonus Question

**How many snacks did Scooby save for you?** _____

Write down the number of times you used the letter E in Part Three. There's your answer!

So, you figured out the first puzzle. Actually, you figured out three puzzles in one. Way to go! Sorry about the snacks.

Read on to find out what happened when we arrived at Ticklewell Manor.

*From the desk of*
**Mystery, Inc.**

As we drove up the long, circular driveway toward the Ticklewell mansion, my head started spinning. This place was huge, not to mention scary. The trees looked like they had all died. I saw crows circling overhead.

"Jeepers!" Daphne cried, shivering. "No wonder there's a ghost haunting this place. It's creepy central."

"The place doesn't look the same as it used to," Fred said. "They've really let it fall apart."

The roof was missing shingles, the wall around the house was crumbling, and there was a broken window.

"On the phone," Fred explained, "Myr-

Welcome to Spookyville

na said that she doesn't want to sell the place—but she doesn't feel like she has a choice."

"What's that supposed to mean?" asked Daphne.

I didn't know much about the family or their factory, but I had a funny feeling that there really was terrible trouble at Ticklewell. That's my Velma Sense, and a good detective always trusts his or her hunches.

We rang the doorbell to the mansion and Myrna Ticklewell answered the door.

"You're here!" she cried, throwing her arms

Myrna Ticklewe ←

Lady of the M...

in the air. She grabbed Fred and hugged him. "Thank you for coming. It's been too long."

"We're glad to be here," Fred said.

"When you called," Myrna said, "I was feeling so desperate. I was all torn up about selling the place, but then I decided it was best. But now no one will buy it. Not with the . . ."

She leaned in toward us very close and

spoke in barely a whisper.

"Not with the ghost," she said, looking over her shoulder.

"G-g-ghost?" Shaggy said.

"Rhost?" Scooby yelped.

Everyone shuddered.

"Oh, this place is terribly cursed," Myrna sighed. She looked like she would cry. "I feel like giving up."

"Don't give up!" Fred said.

"We're here to help," I said.

As we stood there, a man with bushy eyebrows appeared wearing a dark suit and carrying an oversized tray.

"Tea, madam?" the man said in a low, deep voice.

"Sneed!" Myrna cried. "Please meet my old friends. Kids, this is our family butler, Mr. Saul Sneed. He's been with us for years."

"Forever, madam," Mr. Sneed said. "Snack?"

He extended his silver tray of cookies and tea. But as soon as Shaggy and Scooby lunged for a bite, Mr. Sneed yanked it back. They fell into a heap on the floor.

"I'm terribly sorry," Mr. Sneed said. "But we don't serve dogs."

"So, Mr. Sneed," Fred said, circling the butler. "How do you feel about the sale of

Ticklewell Manor?"

"I don't wish to leave," Mr. Sneed sneered. "But if Madam sells, I suppose I shall be forced to go. Unless I find some way to convince her otherwise."

His voice dropped. It sounded like a thinly-veiled threat.

"Oh, Mr. Sneed, stop that talk!" Myrna

Saul Sneed —

The Butler

gave him an astonished look. "You're making the kids nervous. Of course we'll get through this together."

"Oh?" Sneed scowled.

"Mr. Sneed, have you seen the Ghost Knight everyone's talking about?" I asked him.

"Knight? Ghost?" Mr. Sneed scowled. "Hmmmph! I need to get into the kitchen."

With that, he grabbed his tray and left the room.

Myrna turned to us. "I'm sorry if he appears a bit rude," she explained. "Ever since he found out about my decision to sell, he hasn't been himself. But I trust him. Really I do."

No sooner had Mr. Sneed departed when a young woman came into the room. It looked like she was headed to a party. She wore a long, red feather boa.

"Let me introduce my niece, Chloe Clutter," Myrna said. "She's an artist."

Chloe smiled politely. "You have to excuse me," she said. "I haven't been myself lately. I'm just so upset about the manor."

Chloe grabbed Fred's arm. "Hold on! Aren't you Fred Jones?"

"Yes, I am. Wow! Chloe?" Fred said with a mile-wide grin. "What are you doing here?"

Ms. Chloe Clutte

The Nie

"What are *you* doing here?" Chloe asked.

"Helping your Aunt Myrna," Fred said. "We're Mystery, Inc. We solve capers."

"Capers. Whoa. So, you're a detective? Gee, Aunt Myrna must be glad to see you. She's trying so hard to sell this place, but lately it's been a little difficult because —"

All at once, Chloe gasped. She broke off in dramatic sobs.

"Oh, dear. What's wrong?" Daphne asked.

Chloe sniffled loudly. "I wish I could help my Aunt Myrna save this place. I feel so helpless!"

"Where will you go if Ticklewell is sold?" I asked.

"Nowhere!" Chloe exclaimed.

She blew her nose and Shaggy, who had been standing nearby, was instantly drenched.

"Ew, like, I knew I should have worn my rain gear," Shaggy said.

"If you want to help my aunt," Chloe said, holding up a small green business card, "you may want to talk to this man. He's the one who's been pressuring Aunt Myrna to sell the place to the highest bidder. Every time he comes by, he leaves a pile of these dumb cards."

I looked at the business card and then passed it around for everyone to see.

**RIGHT ON REALTY**
Hart Chance, Broker

"Like, I can dig a groovy realtor called 'Right On!'" Shaggy said.

"Maybe we should take a chance with Chance," Daphne added with a giggle.

"Very funny, you two," I said.

Before I could pocket the business card, Chloe grabbed it back from me.

"In case you need to reach me," she said, fighting back more tears, "let me give you my cell phone number."

"Okay, Chloe," Fred said. "Thanks."

Chloe fished in her pocket and pulled out a silver pen. It had her initials, "CC," engraved on it.

"I will do anything I can," Chloe said dramatically, "to help my aunt do the right thing. Anything."

Then she scribbled her number on the back of the green card and handed it to Fred.

"Buh-bye," Daphne said. "Nice meeting you."

"Yeah, like, see you around the mansion, Chloe," Shaggy said.

As she walked away, I rubbed my chin. "She's super nice," I said. "But I think she's hiding something."

"And that butler definitely has something to hide, too," Fred said.

Entry #2

We'd only been at Ticklewell Manor for an hour, but I think we've already met someone who seems extra suspicious! Before we go any further, solve this puzzle to find out the name of the first suspect.

# Puzzle #2

We've put together a list of key words from our first day at the mansion. Circle those words in the letters below. Once every word has been circled, unscramble the remaining letters to spell out the name of our first suspect.

| ARMOR | CARDS | FEATHER | HELP | MYSTERY |
| BOA | ESTATE | GHOST | KNIGHT | PILLOWS |
| BUTLER | FACTORY | HAUNTED | MANSION | TEA |

```
      F           Y
      A D E T N U A H R
      C E   S T E A E       C S
      T L S   O     T     C
    O   T   H   S     W
  O R     A   G Y   O K
      Y       T     M L   N
    N     T F   E   L A   I
  L   O   H E       I R     G
  E     I A     P M   E   H P
      A T S     O         T L
    O H   N   R S D R A C   E
  B E       A         C U H
  R           M         T
        R     B U T L E R
```

The suspect is: _ _ _ _ _ _   _ _ _ _ _ _ _ _

Fred really believed that the butler did it. But t
just seemed too obvious to me. The butler always do
it. Right?

If you solved the word search puzzle correctly,
you know that I suspect Chloe more than anyone e
we've met so far. She's our first suspect!

*From the desk of*
**Mystery, Inc.**

Myrna met us on the top floor of Ticklewell Manor for our official tour. I kept my eyes open for any random clues we might find along the way. There was so much to see in this old place!

Fred asked Myrna to show us the different places in the house where people had seen the Ghost Knight.

"Chloe saw him in the main hallway," Myrna said. We went there first, but didn't find anything.

"Let's step into the parlor," Myrna suggested. "The Ghost Knight appeared to me there last Wednesday."

Just then the doorbell rang.

"You have a visitor, Ms. Ticklewell," Mr.

Is it just me, or does this guy look familiar?

Sneed announced over the intercom system. "The usual visitor."

"Presenting Mr. Hart Chance," Myrna said as we entered the parlor. "Kids, this is my real estate broker. He's handling the sale of the mansion."

"Gee whiz, Myrna, why haven't you returned any of my calls?" Hart blurted. He looked us over, fiddling with something in his pocket.

"Oh, Hart," Myrna winked. "Don't take it personally. I just haven't had a chance to call you back. Get it? Chance?"

"Very funny, Myrna," he said, but he wasn't really laughing.

I crossed my arms and gave him a good, long stare. I hoped that would make him feel even more uncomfortable than he already did. There was something shifty about this guy.

"Mr. Chance," I asked in my most serious, detective-y tone of voice. "Have you met the ghost haunting Ticklewell Manor?"

"Ghost? Here?" Hart laughed out loud. "Aw, I don't believe in that hooey."

"No?" Daphne asked. "Why not?"

"Ghosts can't be real," Hart said with a wink. "At least that's what I keep telling my clients."

"What clients?" Fred asked.

Hart shot Myrna a funny look and then looked back at us. I could tell he felt a little hot under the collar. "Hey, what's going on here?" he stammered.

rt Chance →

he Real Estate
Broker

"Why haven't you found a proper buyer for Ticklewell yet?" Fred asked.

"Proper? I don't know. I guess no one's in the market for a pillow factory. Although we did get one terrific offer . . ."

"He's talking about Charlton Crank at Crank Construction," Myrna interrupted. "But all they want to do is demolish the place to build condos."

"I assure you, Mrs. Ticklewell, it's a good, firm offer," Hart said.

"And a good commission for you?" I asked.

I knew his type. This guy was looking for some cash. He didn't care about the Ticklewell family in the least, even though he pretended to.

Hart shifted on his feet and nervously dug around in his pocket again, but before I could ask a follow-up question, he handed me a neat stack of the green business cards with his name on them.

"Look, kids, I've got to run, but I'm available for all kinds of sales, if you're in the market. You never know when a realtor can come in handy," he quipped before dashing out of the mansion.

I scratched my head and handed the cards to Daphne. "A sales pitch?" I asked. "To us?"

Entry #2

"How weird was that?" Daphne said, stuffing the cards into an envelope.

"Like, weirdo weird," Shaggy said. "That's the kind of weird that makes me . . ."

"Don't say it, Scoob!" Fred warned. He knew what punch line was coming.

"RUNGRY!" Scooby howled with a laugh.

Scooby and Shaggy wandered out of the parlor into the billiard room and started to shoot a game of pool. Just as I was about to check on them, Scooby howled. Shaggy screamed. We all went running into the billiard room.

There, on the other side of the glass doors leading to the garden, stood a dark, brooding man. Scooby and Shaggy huddled together.

"Who are YOU?" I asked. But he couldn't hear me. The doors were closed.

Myrna threw open the glass doors. "Hello, Mr. Wilton," she said. The air rushed inside and blew a chill across the room. "Won't you come in? We have visitors."

"I hate visitors," Mr. Wilton said. His face had a criss-cross of scars from forehead to chin. He looked like Frankenstein's older brother.

"Mr. Wilton, mind your manners!" Myrna

said. "I have an idea. Take them to the Gallery of Armor."

Mr. Wilton grunted. He wasn't big on words.

Daphne leaned over to me and whispered in my

Old Mr. Wilton →

The Caretaker

Entry #2

ear. "I think this guy invented creepy!"

Mr. Wilton led us down a narrow hallway
to a wide set of doors. The doors creaked
loudly as he opened them. Inside were suits
of armor lined up against the wall and win-
dows.

"Oh, what a knight!" Fred joked, pointing
to one hunk of metal.

"Like, this is far-out! Is it okay if we
touch it?" Shaggy asked.

Wilton grunted and this time it sounded
like a "yes," so Shaggy donned one of the
helmets. Scooby modeled a chain metal vest
and sword.

"Be careful!" Myrna cautioned us. "This
is a collection of pieces from my grandfather and his grandfather before him. Mr.
Wilton here is the official armor polisher
of the estate. If something happens to the
armor, Mr. Wilton gets very angry."

"Yeah, let's be careful," I said. I, for
one, didn't want to see Mr. Wilton angry.

Mr. Wilton walked over to the corner of
the armor gallery. As he did, a green business card dropped to the floor.

"Mr. Wilton, I think you dropped this,"
Fred said handing the card back to him. Mr.
Wilton took the card, shoved it into his

pocket, and skulked off wordlessly.

Mr. Hart Chance wasn't exactly Mr. Nice Guy, and Old Mr. Wilton looked like Frankenstein, whic makes him suspicious in my book.

So, after some serious thinking, I've figured o which one of them is our second suspect. Solve the puzzle on the next page to find out.

Entry #2

# Puzzle #3

The following pairs of words have something in common: another word! Can you guess what it is? Use the hints to help you solve it. The first one is done for you.

**BASE**
B A L L
**ROOM**
Hint: Round, bounce, toy

**SNOW**
_ _ _ _ _
**HOUSE**
Hint: color, opposite of black

**HOT**
_ _ _ _ _ _ _ _ _
**CAKE**
Hint: Chips, fudge, candy

**SWAMP**
_ _ _ _ _ _ _
**TRUCK**
Hint: big, ugly creature

**SOCK**
_ _ _ _ _ _
**BUSINESS**
Hint: Bananas, jungle, animal

**FAT**
_ _ _
**GLOSS**
Hint: smile, mouth, pink

### Shaded Letters: _ _ _ _ _ _

### Mr. _ _ _ _ _ _

If you finished the puzzle on the preceding pa[ge], you know that our second suspect is Mr. Wilton. Anyone that grumpy deserves to be watched.

Check out the next case files entry to see what happened when we investigated more of the Tickle[r] Estate.

## From the desk of Mystery, Inc.

We left the armor gallery and walked through a hall, through a set of doors, and outside onto a giant porch. I noticed a brick building in the distance.

"That's where the pillows are made, right?" I asked aloud.

Daphne nodded. "It's the factory," she said, "home of the Perfectly Posh Pillow."

"We'll have to go and check it out," I added.

But Shaggy didn't want to go. "I told you I'm not visiting some ghost factory!" he wailed.

Then I got an idea.

"Daphne and Fred, you go over to the factory and see who's there. Shaggy, Scooby, and I will look for suspects here inside the mansion."

"Now you're talking, Velma!" Daphne said with enthusiasm. "We can meet up later and compare notes."

"Absolutely," I said as Fred and Daphne walked across the lawn to the factory.

Scooby and Shaggy wasted no time. As soon as we walked back inside the Manor they wanted to check out the kitchen.

"Like, to snack or not to snack," Shaggy announced with dramatic flair. "THAT is the question!"

"Reeeee heeee heee!" Scooby laughed, striking a funny pose.

"You guys aren't going anywhere," I said, grabbing Scooby by his collar. I had to put my foot down. "We've got a mystery to solve!"

Suddenly a large woman with red hair came into the room.

"I didn't know Myrna had visitors!" she said. "I'm Deirdre Lux. I live just a hop, skip, and a jump down the road."

"Hello," I said, extending my hand. "I'm Velma Dinkley, and this is Shaggy and Scoo-by-Doo. We're Mystery, Inc."

Deidre Lux

The Next-Door Neighbor

"Oooh! Mystery? How exciting!" she said, snapping her gum. "By the way, you can call me Dee. And if it's information you're looking for, I know just about everything that goes on inside this place."

"Everything?" I said.

Dee Lux smirked. "I keep my eyes open for trouble, and these Ticklewells are all big trouble if you ask me. The way they let the place go! What a disgrace. There are always people coming and going, and the noise! I had to call the police on them once.

"I tell you, things sure would be different if I ran Ticklewell Manor. I've got half a mind to buy this old place and fix it up. I've got quite a nest egg saved up, ya know."

I didn't know, but I was starting to understand. "What about the ghost?" I asked her. "Aren't you afraid of it?

"Ghost?" Dee got a serious look on her face. "Can't say I've ever heard of one around here."

"Can't say?" I asked. "Or won't say?"

Dee looked flustered. Just then, Myrna came into the room with Mr. Sneed and a tray of refreshments. "Dee, what are you doing here?" she asked.

"Uh-oh! I better dash!" Dee said. "See you all later!"

And with that, she raced out of the room.

I was about to chase after her when someone else yelled across the room, "Hold it right there!"

The front door swung wide open, revealing

a man in a sharp-looking suit.

Shaggy and Scooby scrambled behind an enormous chair.

"Mr. Crank! You can't come barging in like this!" Mr. Sneed yelled.

Crank snapped open his case, produced a contract, and handed Myrna a silver pen monogrammed with the initials "CC". It looked very much like the pen that Chloe Cutter had. "You need to sign on the dotted line. Now."

Myrna glanced at the papers and frowned. "Mr. Crank," she sighed. "I think I may have changed my mind."

"WHAT?" Crank cried. "You can't do that."

"Why can't she?" I asked, leaning in close to him.

"Because, well, because..." Mr. Crank stuttered, slicking back his hair. "Who are you?" he asked me.

"Velma Dinkley," I said. "My friends and I are here to help Myrna."

"The best way you can help Myrna is by telling her to sell this old rat trap. I'm ready to take it off her hands right now.

"It's haunted, for Pete's sake!" Crank cried. "She'll be lucky if she finds anyone

Charlton Crank

President, Crank Construction

else to buy the place."

"Maybe you're right," Myrna said, exasperated. "But I don't know if I can sell it."

"Well, you'd better figure it out!" Mr. Crank said angrily. He turned on his heels and slammed the door.

Charlton Crank seemed super pushy, but was he just doing his job? After all, Myrna did promise him the place. What about Dee? Being a nosy neighbor isn't a crime, but she did seem overly attached to Ticklewell Manor. Maybe she's the one who's up to no good?

Solve the puzzle — and find out the name of our final suspect.

# Puzzle #4

Are you any good at cracking codes? Follow the instructions in both parts of this puzzle to figure out the name of your final suspect.

## Part One

This super-secret code was created just for you. In the chart below, each letter of the alphabet has a corresponding number. Use the questions on the next page to help you fill in the missing numbers. Then you can crack the crypto code!

| A | B | C | D | E | F | G | H | I | J | K | L | M |
|---|---|---|---|---|---|---|---|---|---|---|---|---|
| 2 |   | 1 |   |   | 24 |   | 9 |   | 4 |   | 3 |   |

| N | O | P | Q | R | S | T | U | V | W | X | Y | Z |
|---|---|---|---|---|---|---|---|---|---|---|---|---|
|   |   | 13 | 8 |   |   |   | 16 | 17 | 19 |   |   | 23 |

**What Ticklewell Manor room suits a knight best?**

$\overline{22}$ $\overline{2}$ $\overline{3}$ $\overline{3}$ $\overline{26}$ $\overline{11}$ $\overline{18}$　$\overline{21}$ $\overline{24}$

$\overline{2}$ $\overline{11}$ $\overline{12}$ $\overline{21}$ $\overline{11}$

**What kind of neighbor is Dee?**

$\overline{40}$ $\overline{26}$ $\overline{15}$ $\overline{20}$ $\overline{-}$　$\overline{5}$ $\overline{21}$ $\overline{21}$ $\overline{11}$

$\overline{10}$ $\overline{26}$ $\overline{25}$ $\overline{22}$ $\overline{9}$ $\overline{14}$ $\overline{21}$ $\overline{11}$

**Fluffy stuff at the pillow factory that originally came from birds?**

$\overline{24}$ $\overline{26}$ $\overline{2}$ $\overline{20}$ $\overline{9}$ $\overline{26}$ $\overline{11}$ $\overline{7}$

**Shaggy and Scooby's favorite time?**

$\overline{7}$ $\overline{10}$ $\overline{2}$ $\overline{1}$ $\overline{6}$　$\overline{20}$ $\overline{25}$ $\overline{12}$ $\overline{26}$

# Part Two

Use your math smarts to solve the equations below. Put the answers on the middle line. Then plug those numbers into your cryptogram chart. Put the corresponding letters on the bottom line. They will spell out the name of the third suspect.

$8-7$　$3(3)$　$203-201$　$242/22$　$1+9-7$　$10 \times 3-10$　$7 \times 3$　$3+8-1$

$\_\_$　$\_\_$　$\_\_$　$\_\_$　$\_\_$　$\_\_$　$\_\_$　$\_\_$

$\_\_$　$\_\_$　$\_\_$　$\_\_$　$\_\_$　$\_\_$　$\_\_$　$\_\_$

$0/10$　$1+9+1$　$\frac{1}{2} \times 4$　$5 \times 2$　$94-90+2$

$\_\_$　$\_\_$　$\_\_$　$\_\_$　$\_\_$　← *Numbers*

$\_\_$　$\_\_$　$\_\_$　$\_\_$　$\_\_$　← *Letters*

From his grouchy comments, Charlton seems like he's got a few grudges and maybe an evil plan or two up his sleeve. Now that we've got all our suspects in line, we're ready to start the serious task of collecting clues.

## From the desk of Mystery, Inc.

Later that night, Daphne and Fred came back from the pillow factory with nothing to show except a couple of feathers stuck to their shoes. They hadn't seen anything mysterious — yet. Of course Shaggy, Scooby, and I hadn't seen much mystery either. We told them about the strange encounter with Myrna, Dee, and Mr. Crank.

"Gosh, that Charlton Crank sounds like one bad guy," Fred said. "Good thing I'm back to help catch him."

The sky got darker, and I knew it was time for dinner. We'd hardly eaten anything all day. I could hear Scooby's stomach rumbling like an engine.

Myrna invited us to stay for supper and

continue our investigation that night. Maybe we'd see the Ghost Knight with our own eyes? Maybe we could even catch one of the suspects, too? Just thinking about it gave me Velma Tingles all over.

Mr. Sneed prepared a delicious dinner of spaghetti and meatballs, one of my personal favorites.

Shaggy inhaled fistfuls of noodles while Scooby juggled three meatballs right into his mouth. Suddenly, the lights went out!

"HELP!" Myrna screamed.

Ready to Chow Down

I noticed a faint glowing shape in the room. Then, I saw a pair of bright red eyes. Suddenly, the lights came back on. When I saw what was standing at the other end of the dining table, I wished that they hadn't. It was the Ghost Knight. His suit of armor was glowing ominously.

"Myrna Ticklewell, BEWARE!" it bellowed. "I am the ghost of Thadeus Ticklewell! Woe and misery to anyone who dares to sell the Ticklewell estate."

"It's the Ghost Knight!" Myrna screamed.

"Wooooooooooo!" yelled the Ghost Knight as it lurched noisily toward Shaggy and Scooby.

"Like, r-r-r-run!" Shaggy howled. "F-f-f-fast!"

Scooby and Shaggy high-tailed it out of the dining room. The Ghost Knight was in hot pursuit, armor clanging. Scooby and Shaggy scooted around a corner, into the hallway, and then around another corner, back into the dining room. Fred, Daphne, Myrna, Sneed, and I hustled into the hall and then — BLAM! Everyone collided.

"Jeepers!" Daphne cried.

"Creepers!" Fred added.

Entry #5

"That was a close call," Sneed said.

"Hey! Wait a minute. Where's the ghost?" I asked.

He was gone.

Myrna rubbed her chin. "Listen! . . . In the drawing room. Do you hear that?"

We went into the drawing room, but there was no sound anymore.

"Are my ears playing tricks on me?" Myrna mused. "I swore that I heard a noise."

Suddenly, Chloe ran into the room, breathless.

"The knight! The knight!" she exclaimed.

"Where? Where?" I asked. We were all scratching our heads at that point.

"Down — the — hall — help — I — can't —" Chloe could hardly get the words out.

Shaggy took one step back. "Whoa, Chloe! You look like you just saw a—"

"RHOST!" Scooby said. He gulped. "Ruh roh."

"Hey!" Fred shouted enthusiastically from the other side of the room, "Over here! I think I found our first real clue!"

Before we all rushed over to see what it was, I snapped the photo below. Examine it and see if you can find the clue that Fred saw.

What a mess!

Entry #5

# Puzzle #5

## Part One

Below are some phrases that the gang might say. Fill in the missing letters for each unfinished word. Those letters will make up the tiles that will help us figure out the clue.

"Shaggy and Scooby, clean up your room. It's a huge ME☐☐☐!"

"Like, solving mysteries is totally ☐☐OOVY!"

"Jinkies! I see a ☐☐GN up ahead and it says WATCH OUT!"

"Someone give a Scooby a BO☐☐ before he slurps up the place!"

"Hold on to your seats, gang. This is going to be one S☐☐RY ride!"

"What's wrong, Daphne? You look like you've S☐☐☐ a ghost!"

"Man, like no one understands how HA☐☐ it is being monster bait!"

"Like, someone put some HAM☐☐RGERS on the grill. I'm starving!"

## Part Two

Put the letter tiles into this box and unscramble them to spell out the first clue.

## The First Clue:

Congratulations on finding the business card! Now we are one step closer to breaking this case wide open. You're a pro! All that attention to detail is really starting to show, gumshoe.

*From the desk of*
**Mystery, Inc.**

Sneed brought me and Daphne to one room (for the girls), while Shaggy, Scooby, and Fred went into another room (for the boys) a few paces down the hallway.

"Um, Mr. Sneed?" I asked as he led us inside and turned down the blankets.

Sneed leaned forward and peered down at me. "Is there a problem?"

"Yes," I blurted, "well, not exactly. Except that there is, well, have you worn any armor lately?"

Mr. Sneed looked annoyed by the question. "I don't wear armor," he snapped. "That's a preposterous thing to ask! Besides, I'm allergic to something in the armor metal. It makes me break out in gigantic, puffy hives."

"Eeeeew, gross," Daphne said.

It was kind of gross to think about Sneed's hives, but I was happy to hear that the allergy ruled him out of our list of suspects.

A few minutes after Sneed left, Shaggy and Scooby showed up outside our door.

"Like, wh-wh-what are we still doing in this place?" Shaggy asked, shaking so hard I could hear his knees knock.

"Ret's ro! Ret's ro!" Scooby said, teeth chattering.

"We can't!" I declared. "Not now. We have to be here when the ghost comes back. Let's just get some sleep, and we'll continue our search in the morning. We can take turns keeping watch tonight in case someone, or something shows up."

"S-s-s-shows up?" Shaggy said. "Like, what do you mean?"

"Shaggy, don't forget, we're Mystery, Inc. We don't run away from mysteries, we solve them," I said.

"Okay," Shaggy said. "Like, I'll try to calm down."

"Actually, why don't you get up and get

another snack?" I suggested. "I saw some triple-whip cream pie down in the kitchen."

"Rowf!" Scooby barked. I could almost see the happy little thought bubbles over his head with dancing salamis and flying sandwiches. "Mmmmmmmm," he said, rubbing his belly. "Rounds rood!"

Daphne, Fred, and I waited for Shaggy and Scooby to come back from the kitchen, but they were taking an unusually long time. Then I heard a loud crash.

"Was that what I think it was?" Daphne said.

We made a mad dash for the Manor kitchen, sure that we'd find the Ghost Knight inside. But as soon as we entered, I saw the source of the clatter. Scooby and Shaggy were sitting in a pile of pans.

"Ruh roh," Scooby said. "Ree hee hee."

"Like, we knocked over the shelf," Shaggy said, stifling his own giggles.

"Talk about pandemonium," I said, cracking a bad joke.

While Daphne, Fred, and I searched the room for signs of the ghost, Shaggy and Scooby searched for the sandwich fixings. They found all the ingredients to make themselves double-decker burgers with mayonnaise, anchovies, and chocolate chips on top. Scooby went into a pantry to look for even more toppings.

Crash! Crash! Clank!

"Did you hear that?" Fred asked.

Shaggy yelled out in the direction of the pantry, "Like, Scooby, could you please cool it with the pans? Can't a man eat a double-decker burger in peace?"

Crash! Crash! Clank!

"Scoob, just stop it with the pans!" Shaggy cried.

Scooby poked his head out of the pantry.

"Rhat rans?" he asked. He was holding an enormous jar of pickles.

"I thought I heard the ghost," I said.

"Me, too!" Daphne said. "I heard noise coming from inside that door!"

We scuttled over to a large blue door next to the pantry. All was quiet now. Bravely, Fred stood at the front of our group and turned the knob.

"Come out and see us, Mr. Ghost Knight," he said as he pulled the door open.

I held my breath. We all did.

But as the door flung open, a hundred cans of beans came crashing down onto Fred's head.

"Yeeowch," he mumbled, rubbing his temple. "That hurts."

"Sorry you got beaned," Daphne joked. "But look what I found here on the floor."

I think we just found the second clue! Can you tell what it is? Solve the puzzle on the next page to find out for sure.

# Puzzle #6

## Part One

Find the missing letters! The difference between the words in columns **A** and **C** is just **ONE** letter. Identify that missing letter to fill in column **B**. When you are done, move on to part two.

| A | B | C |
|---|---|---|
| SELF | | FILES |
| RAG | | RAGE |
| LEARN | | LEAN |
| EVIL | | OLIVE |
| TREE | | EGRET |
| LAID | | LID |
| TEARS | | MASTER |
| OAR | | ROAD |
| SPIDER | | RIDES |
| SWEAR | | ANSWER |
| CHINS | | SNITCH |
| BAR | | BEAR |
| PEEL | | SLEEP |
| SCRAPE | | PEARS |
| SEAL | | SCALE |

Entry #6

## Part Two

Now, transfer the letters (in order) from column **B** into the missing spaces below. **Ta da!** You've got clue two!

A S_LV_ _

M_N O_R_M_E_ _E_

WITH THE LE_T_R_

_ _ ON THE SIDE

You found the second clue: a silver pen with the initials CC on the side. But don't stop now! Read on to see what happens when Fred and Daphne investigate strange noises down in the parlor and get my next big, bright idea.

*From the desk of*
**Mystery, Inc.**

After we left the kitchen, Fred and Daphne went off to check for clues in the parlor, while I roamed the halls with Shaggy and Scooby. Everyone was tired, but no one could sleep; not with a ghost on the loose!

As we walked along a long hallway, I paused to look out of a large window. I could see the factory across the lawn.

"Hey!" I cried. "Look! Over there!"

Shaggy and Scooby ran over and looked out of the window with me.

"Look at the Ticklewell factory! There's a light!" I yelled. "Someone must be inside. Do you think it might be the..."

"Rhost?" Scooby asked with a gulp.

I nodded. "We have to go and check it out."

Reluctantly, Shaggy and Scooby followed me downstairs, out the side door, and across the lawn to the factory.

I was surprised to find that someone had pushed the door ajar. It was wedged open with a small stack of green business cards.

"Hmmmm," I thought aloud.

"Zoinks! Like, I think we should turn around and head back to the house," Shaggy muttered.

"Shhhhh!" I said, putting my finger up to my lips. "We have to be very quiet or some-one will hear us. We're not going anywhere except into that factory. I just know we'll find another clue in there!"

We walked quickly and quietly through the door and to the main assembly line floor. Of course, the equipment was all shut down, but the light I'd seen from the house was on. A single, yellow bulb dangled from the ceiling.

"Like, could this place be any freakier?" Shaggy asked.

I chuckled. "Let's have a look around," I suggested. "Someone left on this light, and I have a sneaking suspicion that it just might be our knight!"

"So, like, does that make it a knight light?" Shaggy asked, giggling to himself.

"Reee hee hee," Scooby laughed.

We searched under tables and inside cabinets, looking for something — anything — that might lead us to the ghost. We came across a row of giant, funny-looking vats. Shaggy stuck his hand into one bin. He pulled out a handful of gray and white feathers.

"Look at these!" he cried, laughing. "Zoinks! There must be a lot of naked chickens running around here somewhere."

I laughed out loud, and then stuck my own hand into another bin of feathers. Soon, Scooby joined in. Shaggy snapped this photo of our feather fight!

"Now try and catch me!" Shaggy cried, turning to run away. Unfortunately, he caught his sneaker on the floor and went flying into yet another bin of feathers.

"Aaaaaaah!" Shaggy cried. He landed in the bin face-first.

Suddenly, the entire factory room went black.

"Rello?" Scooby asked into the darkness.

"Hey, Scoob!" Shaggy cried. "Like, who turned out the lights?"

Entry #7

Always ready to lend a hand...

"The light bulb must have blown out," I said. "Shaggy, are you still in the feather bin?"

"Uh-huh," Shaggy said. "I feel like someone just plucked me."

"Reeeheeheee!" Scooby let out a funny little laugh.

"Are you laughing at me?" Shaggy asked.

"Reeeheeheee! Rop rickling ree!" Scooby cried.

"Tickling you?" Shaggy said. "What are you talking about, Scoob? No one's tickling you. I'm all the way over here, remember?"

"Ruh roh."

At that exact moment, I found my spare

flashlight and shone a bright beam onto the scene. The yellow light cast a glow across Scooby's face. Just as I feared, Scooby, Shaggy, and I were not alone. That No-Good Knight was standing right there! He was the one who'd been tickling Scooby.

Shaggy took a flying leap out of the feather bin and ran. Scooby and I knocked into another bin sending a pile of feathers flying into the air. There were feathers everywhere. It was like a snowstorm of fluff, and I couldn't see a thing.

The knight was following us, though. I

could hear the clanking of his armor.

"Run!" Scooby said.

It felt like we were running fast, but not getting anywhere. What was going on?

There was a loud thump and then the sound of whirring motors. I realized we were stuck on one of the assembly line conveyor belts moving straight into a noisy machine. I shone my flashlight at it and read a sign on its side: "SUPER-DUPER FEATHER CRUSHER."

"Feather crusher?" cried Shaggy.

"We need to get off!" I said. "NOW!"

But before I could say jump, the conveyor belt came to a sudden halt, and the lights went on. The knight was gone, and Daphne and Fred were now standing where he had been.

"Thank goodness you're here! Did you see the Ghost Knight?" I asked them.

They both shrugged. "What's going on?"

"Like, the Ghost Knight was going to get us!" Shaggy said.

"It looks more like a truckload of birds were going to get you," Daphne said.

I couldn't believe that the ghost had gotten away again. What was I doing wrong?

Then I saw something fantastic on the floor. "Another clue! Another clue!" I cried, pointing.

"Velma, all I see are a whole lot of feathers," Daphne said.

"Exactly!" I said.

If you examine the picture we took, you'll see I wasn't totally featherbrained! Can you guess what the final clue is? If not, solve the puzzle!

# Puzzle #7

Everything on this Scooby and Shaggy menu is all mixed-up. Help the gang make sense of these scrambled food items. Fill in the blanks. Then unscramble the shaded letters to reveal your third clue.

S_ _ AMI SANDWICH

_ _ _ ESE STICKS

HAMBU_ G_ _

_ OUGHNU_

PI_ K_ _ S

FRENCH _ _ IE_

**Shaded Letters:** _ _ _ _ _ _ _ _ _ _ _

**The Third Clue:** _ _ _ _ _ _ _ _ _ _

They don't call it Ticklewell Manor for nothing! It's all about the feathers. With three suspects and three clues in hand, the pieces of this mystery are finally coming together.

*From the desk of*
**Mystery, Inc.**

"Okay, everyone, listen up," Fred said. "Now that we found this red feather, I know what we need to do!

"I think we should try to trap the No-Good Knight in action," Fred said, "using Shaggy and Scooby as ghost bait!"

"Like, no way, Fred! I'm not bait like some squirmy worm!"

"Ree reither!" seconded Scooby.

Daphne pasted on her widest, brightest smile. "Oh, Scooby and Shaggy," she cooed. "I just got these free passes to the Ice Cream Factory, and they're having an all-you-can-eat festival later this week."

"Rippppeee!" cried Scooby.

"But no ice cream until we catch that

Fred's no featherbrain!

ghost," Daphne clarified.

Shaggy and Scooby exchanged looks.

"Well," Shaggy said decisively, "what are we waiting for? Next stop, Ice Cream City."

"Rum-rum!" Scooby added, tossing a few feathers into the air.

We headed back to the Manor to get ready. Our destination was the Gallery of Armor. We figured that would be the ideal place to lure the ghost. We told Myrna all about the plan, too. But no one else knew, not even Mr. Sneed.

The gallery seemed extra-dark, even with the lights on. Daphne and I clung together, arms linked.

"Did this place just get creepier?" she asked.

I nodded. "I hope Fred's plan works. If my calculations are correct, we have a seventy-percent chance of success."

"Like, I hope it's better than that!" Shaggy wailed.

Daphne used her best fashion skills to help Shaggy and Scooby choose suits of armor. She chose a suit of armor that made Shaggy look bigger than he was. Scooby put on a helmet and an apron made from chain-metal links. They both looked like the real deal as they climbed atop two fake horses in the gallery.

"Too bad we don't have any real horses," Fred said.

"Yeah, like, I guess there aren't any in this neighborhood," Shaggy said, laughing.

"Ree hee hee hoo," Scooby laughed, doing his best horse imitation.

Shaggy and Scooby got into position, and

Entry #8

we got out of sight. Our job was to make a whole lot of noise. We hoped that would attract the attention of the Ghost Knight.

I was carrying a strong magnet that was so supercharged, I could see all the metal objects in the room leaning toward me slightly, even though I'd stored it inside a lead bag.

Scooby and Shaggy raised their lances into the air. They pretended to bob and weave and hit each other for real. Of course, they were laughing the entire time. We cheered and broke into a chorus of "ooooohs" and

Sir Shaggy and
Sir Scooby

"aaaahs."

It was just past midnight when I heard the door to the gallery creak open. I crouched down with Fred, Daphne, and Myrna asking them to be quiet. Shaggy and Scooby waved their lances into the air to greet whoever had entered the room.

It was the No-Good Knight. He was carrying a lance, too.

So far, everything was going as planned. We were seconds away from catching the Ghost Knight and ending Myrna's misery.

I stood up on the other side of the room and raced across the floor.

The knight looked over at me with surprise and then tried to turn away. He'd figured out that something was going on, but it was too late for the knight to escape!

With one swift motion, I pulled out the supercharged magnet. Instantly, I felt it connect with the knight in scaring armor. He wobbled a bit and then came flying toward the magnetic charge.

The only problem was that the No-Good Knight wasn't the only thing that came toward me. Scooby, Shaggy, the lances, and about fifty other pieces of armor got pulled toward the

Entry #8

super-magnet. I ended up in a giant pile on the floor with a whole lot of metal.

The gang helped me up, and I dusted off my clothes.

At last we were going to take off the helmet to reveal the knight's true identity.

Ghost Busted!

Now we're just waiting for you to put together the mystery's clues, and identify the person who's been haunting Ticklewell Manor. Use the chart on next page to help you. But hurry! We don't want th knight to get away.

# Solve the Mystery

Take the solutions from each of the puzzles and write them in the chart on the next page according to the instructions:

| **SUSPECTS** Write the name of the suspect from each of the puzzles: | **CLUES** Write the clue from each of the puzzles: | | |
|---|---|---|---|
| | Puzzle #5 Solution: _____ | Puzzle #6 Solution: _____ | Puzzle #7 Solution: _____ |
| Puzzle #2 Solution: _____ | | | |
| Puzzle #3 Solution: _____ | | | |
| Puzzle #4 Solution: _____ | | | |

Put an **X** in the suspect's box if he or she can be connected to that clue. When you're done, there should only be one suspect with an **X** in all of their boxes.

Write that person's name here:

_____

Got the name of the ghost? Turn the page to see what happened when we let Myrna unmask the bad guy.

From the desk of
**Mystery, Inc.**

Myrna was nervous as she leaned over the Knight in Scaring Armor. Carefully, she reached for the helmet and lifted it up.

"No!" Myrna screamed. The helmet lid dropped down again. I heard a small, squeaky voice say, "Hey! Ouch! That hurt!"

I bent down and lifted off the entire helmet.

Now everyone could see why Myrna had been so shocked. The Knight in Scaring Armor was a girl — and she was Myrna's own niece.

"Chloe?" Daphne cried.

"Like, how did a girl turn into a knight?" Shaggy asked.

"Easy," I said. "A suit of armor hides everything. Doesn't it, Chloe?"

Chloe threw her hands up and pulled off more of the armor. "I can't believe you figured me out. How did you know?"

I looked Chloe in the eye. "You gave yourself away," I said. "First we knew you were a likely suspect because you had at least one of those green business cards."

Mystery, Inc.
gets their . . .

girl!

"Our second clue was your silver pen, mono-grammed with CC, your initials!" I said.

"Gee, at first I thought that CC was Crank Construction and that Charlton Crank was the bad guy," Daphne said.

"Me, too," I concurred. "And it seemed that way right up until last night in the feather factory."

"Oh, quit squawking! What do I have in common with a bunch of plucked feathers?" Chloe asked.

"Plenty!" I said. "Among those white feath-ers, we found one large red feather, just like the ones on your trademark boa. That final clue eliminated other suspects."

"Impossible!" Chloe cried. "This is ri-diculous! I want my mommy!"

Myrna stepped in. "Your mommy would be very disappointed in your behavior, Chloe," Myrna said. "I've known you since you were born, and I've never seen you act this way. What's come over you? Why would you do this to our family home!"

Chloe's eyes were welling up with tears. She was getting emotional, just as she'd gotten yesterday when we first asked her questions.

"I see how you wore the knight's costume, but how did you get it to glow? And those freaky-tiki eyes? Like, those are scary-licious!" Shaggy said.

"Reah! Rar-ree-ricious!" Scooby said.

Chloe took a deep breath. "I used glow-in-the-dark paint on the suit of armor and glow sticks. I got it all at the craft store."

"Very clever," Fred said.

"I can't believe you would deliberately hurt our family!" Myrna said.

"I didn't mean to hurt anyone!" Chloe exclaimed. "I just wanted to keep our family home. You were going to sell it! I figured if I could just keep away the realtors and the developers . . . I didn't know that the ghost sightings would scare you away, Aunt Myrna. Don't you know that Hart Chance and Charlton Crank don't care about this beautiful old house! All they want is to make money from the property."

"I know that now," Myrna said. She laid her hand on Chloe's shoulder. "All I want is to keep our family — and our family history — together."

Chloe started to cry.

"Isn't there any way that you can save Ticklewell, Myrna, now that you know how Chloe feels?" Daphne asked.

"I remember this place when I was a kid," Fred added. "I would hate to see it go away or get turned into condos."

"So would I," Chloe said, sniffling loudly. "I'm so sorry that I almost blew it. I just didn't think you'd listen to me, Aunt Myrna. No one ever listens to me!"

"I listened to you," I said to Chloe. "Like when you said you'd do anything to help your aunt. At first I thought you meant that in a good way. But later, I knew it meant that you would go to any lengths — even dressing up as a ghostly knight — to get her attention."

"I'd be honored to help you fix up the place, Madam," Mr. Sneed interjected. "If it means I can keep my position."

"Oh!" Myrna wailed. "What would I do without the two of you? Now maybe we can bring back the pillow factory to its glory!"

I clapped my hands together and everyone followed suit. We applauded the big ideas for saving — and not selling — Ticklewell Manor. Everyone celebrated Myrna's promise with a loud cheer. She had her place back. The ghost was gone. And Mystery, Inc. had solved another case.

Scooby and Shaggy got out of the rest of

their armor as fast as they could. Now that the culprit had been unmasked and the mystery explained, it was time for one last thing.

"Ice Cream Factory, here we come!" Shaggy crowed.

"Rummy! Rice ream!" Scooby yelled out.

"Like, what flavor do you want, Scoob? Bubble gum parfait? Or butterfudge ripply-dip?"

"Reah, reah!" Scooby licked his chops. "Ret's ro!"

Rum! Rum! And Away We Go!

"Like, what are we waiting for?" Shaggy grabbed at the air like he was holding an invisible lance.

"Rooby Dooby Doo!" Scooby cried, pretending to grab his own invisible lance.

Together they charged the door.

"Here's to the Knights of Mystery, Inc.!" Fred cried.

"Otherwise known as the Knights in Hungry Armor!" I said with a laugh.

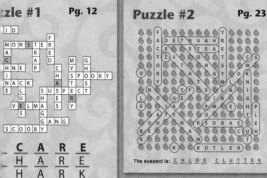

## Puzzle #1 — Pg. 12

Crossword grid (partial):
```
        I D
M O N S T E R       F
A       R           R
C       A           E
H N E   P     C     M G
I       S     H   S P O O K Y
N A C K       A     T
E L     S U S P E C T
    V E L M A     S Y
        S         G
              G A N G
S C O O B Y
```

_ C A R E
_ H A R E
_ H A R K
_ H A C K
_ N A C K

## Puzzle #2 — Pg. 23

The suspect is: C H L O E   C L U T T E R

BASE
**BALL**

ROOM
Hint: Round, bounce, toy

HOT
**CHOCOLATE**

CAKE
Hint: Chips, fudge, candy

SOCK
**MONKEY**

BUSINESS
Hint: Bananas, jungle, animal

SNOW
**WHITE**

HOUSE
Hint: color, opposite of black

SWAMP
**MONSTER**

TRUCK
Hint: big, ugly creature

FAT
**LIP**

GLOSS
Hint: smile, mouth, pink

Shaded Letters: L T N W O I
Mr. W I L T O N

## Puzzle #4 — Pg. 41

```
A B C D E F G H I J K L M N O P Q R S T U V W X Y Z
5 25 24 22 9  25 4  6 3 12 10 21 13 8 11 7 20 16 17 19 15 18 23
```

Picklewell Manor room suits a knight best?
**GALLERY OF**
**ARMOR**

kind of neighbor is Dee?
**NEXT - DOOR**
**NEIGHBOR**

stuff at the factory that originally came from birds?
**FEATHERS**

is the favorite time for Shaggy and Scooby?
**SNACK TIME**

```
(3)  203-201 242/22  1+9-7  10x3-10  7x3  3x8-1
 9    2      21      20     21       10
 H    A      R       L      T        O    N
```

```
9+1  ½x4  5x2  94-90+2
 4   2    10   6
 R   A    N    K
```

## Puzzle #5 — Pg. 47

ME SS
GR OOVY
SI GN
BO NE
CA RY
SE EN
HA RD
BU RGER

G R E E N
B U S I N E S S
C A R D

## Puzzle #6 — Pg. 54

| SELF | I | FILES |
|------|---|-------|
| RAG | E | RAGE |
| LEARN | R | LEAN |
| EVIL | O | OLIVE |
| TREE | G | EGRET |
| LAID | A | LID |
| TEARS | M | MASTER |
| OAR | D | ROAD |
| SPIDER | P | RIDES |
| SWEAR | N | ANSWER |
| CHINS | T | SNITCH |
| BAR | E | BEAR |
| PEEL | S | SLEEP |
| SCRAPE | C | PEARS |
| SEAL | E | SCALE |

A S I L V E R
MON O G R A M M E D  P E N
WITH THE LE T T E R S
C C ON THE SIDE

## Puzzle #7 — Pg. 63

S A L AMI SANDWICH

C H E ESE STICKS

HAMBUR G E R

D OUGHNUT

PIC K L E S

FRENCH FR IES

Shaded Letters: A H E E R D T E F R

The Third Clue: R E D   F E A T H E R

## Solve the Mystery — Pg. 71

| SUSPECTS<br>Write the name of the suspect from each of the puzzles: | CLUES<br>Write the clue from each of the puzzles: | | |
|---|---|---|---|
| | Puzzle #5<br>Solution:<br>BUSINESS CARD | Puzzle #6<br>Solution:<br>MONOGRAMMED PEN | Puzzle #7<br>Solution:<br>RED FEATHER |
| Puzzle #2<br>Solution: CHLOE | X | X | X |
| Puzzle #3<br>Solution: WILTON | X | | |
| Puzzle #4<br>Solution: CRANK | X | X | |